This

Dora the Explorer
Annual

belongs to

BILLIE   PURVIS

....

....

Contents

EGMONT

We bring stories to life

First published in Great Britain 2009 by Egmont UK Limited
239 Kensington High Street, London W8 6SA
Created for Egmont by John Brown
Editorial: Chloe Martin • Design: Liz Adcock

© 2009 Viacom International Inc.
All rights reserved.
Nickelodeon, Nick Jr., Dora the Explorer and all related titles, logos
and characters are trademarks of Viacom International Inc.

ISBN 978 1 4052 4642 2
1 3 5 7 9 10 8 6 4 2
Printed in Italy

Join in every day on Nick Jr.
www.nickjr.co.uk

Star Catcher

Hello! Abuela has just given me a present. It's a Star Pocket – a special place to put Stars. Inside the Star Pocket there is a Star World, where all the Stars can play together. Let's put the Star Pocket on Backpack.

Do you see a Star anywhere? Reach up and catch him!

Yay, we caught him. It's a baby Star. His name is Woo Hoo. He likes to play peekaboo! Let's put him in the Star Pocket.

Uh oh, there's Swiper the fox! Quick, say "Swiper, no swiping!" We were too late. Swiper swiped the Star Pocket and stuck it to a balloon. The balloon is floating away, with Woo Hoo inside the Star Pocket! We need to get it back.

SPANISH

let's go
vámonos
say 'VAH-moh-nohs'

Map says the balloon is going to Cloud Castle. To get there, we need to go across the Stormy Water then over Dragon Mountain. ¡Vámonos!

9

Here's the Stormy Water. Hey, I see Explorer Stars – estrellas! Let's reach up and catch the Stars. Well done, we caught them. There's Saltador, the jumping Star, and Noisy Star, who's very loud! There's Glowy the bright light Star and Switchy, who can change shape! They will all help us to rescue Woo Hoo.

Do you see something here that we can use to get across the Stormy Water? Yes, the boat! Well done.

SPANISH

stars
estrellas
say 'eh-STRAY-yahs'

We're sailing across the Stormy Water. It's very dark here. Maybe one of the Explorer Stars can help us see through the darkness. Which Explorer Star do you think can help? That's right, Glowy! She is lighting the way for us. Thanks, Glowy! Now we can see where we're going.

Oh no, what's that blocking our way? It's a whale! And she's asleep. Which Star can make a lot of noise to wake up the whale? Yes, Noisy Star. Let's help. Say "Honk, honk!" Louder! Great, we woke up the whale and she moved out of the way.

We made it across the Stormy Water. Now let's go over Dragon Mountain. Wow, it's so high! There's Azul the train. He says he will give us a ride over Dragon Mountain.

Hey, there's a pattern in the track. Let's say the shapes out loud. Square, triangle, circle. Square, triangle, circle!

Oh no, there's the dragon! We need to get over the Mountain really fast. But there are some pieces missing from the track. Which Explorer Star can change shape and help us fill in the missing shapes? Switchy, right!

What shape is the first missing piece? Circle, right! Switchy is making a circle shape to fill it in. Which shape should Switchy make to fill in the second piece? A square, yes. Which piece comes third? A triangle!

Hey, the dragon was a friendly dragon! She was just trying to warn us that the shapes were missing. Thank you, dragon. ¡Gracias!

SPANISH

thank you
gracias
say 'GRAH-see-ass'

13

We went across the Stormy Water and over Dragon Mountain. Where do we need to go next? Cloud Castle, right! Do you see it anywhere? Yes, up there! It is very high in the sky.

We need an Explorer Star to help us jump super-high. Who can help us jump? Saltador, right! One, two, three – jump! ¡Salta! Yay, we jumped right up to Cloud Castle.

SPANISH

jump
salta
say 'SAHL-tah'

There's the Prince of Cloud Castle. He has the Star Pocket – with Woo Hoo inside! The Prince will only give it back if we win a Star-catching contest.

We need to be really good Star catchers and save Woo Hoo! Reach up and catch as many Stars as you can! Great, let's see how many Stars we have caught. Count with me – 1, 2, 3, 4, 5, 6, 7, 8. Eight Stars!

The Prince didn't catch any Stars. That means we win the contest! We got the Star Pocket back and rescued Woo Hoo! Thanks very much for all your help.

WE DID IT!
¡LO HICIMOS!

15

Benny the bull is flying in his hot-air balloon! Use the code to colour in the picture.

Azul has got his carriages muddled up! Write over the dotted numbers to show the carriages in order of size from largest to smallest.

Say "Choo choo" just like a train! Well done!

18

Dora and Boots are flying with Tico in his plane! Look at the pictures. Which two are exactly the same?

Answers on page 69.

To the South Pole

¡Hola! Today we've met a little penguin! His name is Pingüino. But he is very hot here. He lives at the South Pole, where it is very cold. Will you help us take Pingüino back to the South Pole? Great. ¡Vámonos! Let's ask Map how to get to the South Pole. Shout "Map!"

Map says that the South Pole is very far away. To get there, we go across the Icy Water and climb over Snowy Mountain.

So first let's go to the Icy Water. Do you see it? Yes, there it is! It is so far away. Do you see something that we can use to fly to the Icy Water?

Yes, the aeroplane - el avión! It's very cold at the South Pole! Before we go, we need to put on some warm clothes.

SPANISH

aeroplane
avión
say 'av-ee-ON'

Draw a circle around each thing that will keep Dora and Boots warm!

Answers on page 69.

Here's the Icy Water. Do you see something that can take us across? Yes, a boat! But it's chained up. Hey, Pingüino has found the key to unlock the boat. Well done, Pingüino!

There's Swiper. Quick, say "Swiper, no swiping!" to stop him taking the key. Oh no, we were too late!

Swiper threw the key into the water. Pingüino can dive down to get it back. Penguins are great swimmers! When you see the key, say "There it is!" Great. Now we can unlock the boat and sail across the Icy Water.

Do you remember where we need to go next? Snowy Mountain, right. Hey, here's a snowmobile! We can use it to get to Snowy Mountain really fast. But we need to watch out for the seals!

Trace a path with your finger all the way to Snowy Mountain, but don't bump into the seals!

Great - we made it all the way to Snowy Mountain!

Answer on page 69.

Snowy Mountain is very slippery. I know, let's follow Pingüino and waddle up the Mountain like penguins! Stand up, then put your arms by your side and waddle like a penguin!

Uh-oh, Snowy Mountain has cracked in two! Boots and Pingüino are stuck on the other side. We need to find a rope to throw to them. Let's check in my Backpack. Say "Backpack!"

Tick ✓ the circle next to the rope!

You found the rope. ¡Excelente!

SPANISH

excellent
excelente
say 'ex-seh-LEN-tay'

Now let's throw the rope. Put your arm in the air and throw the rope towards Boots and Pingüino so they can swing across. Great! Now we can go down the other side of Snowy Mountain!

Here's the South Pole – we made it! There are so many penguins. Pingüino needs to find his mami and papi. Let's help him call to them. Say "Orc, orc!" like a penguin. Hey, Pingüino's mami and papi are calling back to him! Can you see them?

ORC, ORC!

ORC, ORC!

SPANISH

mummy, daddy
mami, papi
say 'MAH-mee,
PAH-pee'

26

Pingüino has found his mami and papi. He is so glad to be home. We did it. ¡Lo hicimos! Thanks for helping. We couldn't have done it without you!

WE DID IT!
¡LO HICIMOS!

27

Woodland Puzzles

Dora is going on a picnic in the woods! Tick ✓ the circle next to each thing that she should take with her.

Boots is coming too – and he's brought some cookies! The cookies are in a square box. The box is red, to match his boots! Can you find the right box?

Answers on page 69.

Draw lines to match the animal shadows into pairs! Then draw a circle around the shadow that doesn't have a pair.

SPANISH

rabbit
conejo
say 'cohn-EH-hoh'

I've met a little rabbit! Twitch your nose like a rabbit, un conejo!

30

This little squirrel is hungry! Which path will lead him to the nuts?

I like eating cupcakes! What is your favourite food?

Answers on page 69.

The Shy Rainbow

Hi! Today we're at Rainbow Rock, looking for rainbows! Do you see a rainbow hiding anywhere? Yes, there's one! Hello, rainbow! The rainbow says his name is Arco Iris.

SPANISH

rainbow
arco iris
say 'AR-koh EAR-ees'

The sun wants Arco Iris to shine in the sky and show his colours to everyone. But Arco Iris is shy. He's never shone in the sky before! Don't worry Arco Iris, we'll help you! Will you help, too? Great!

Arco Iris has such pretty colours. Let's name them – in English and Spanish! What is the first colour? Red, right – rojo. Which colour comes next? It's blue – azul. Then green – verde. And which colour is last? Yellow, yes. Amarillo!

We need to get to Rainy Mountain. Who do we ask for help when we don't know where to go? Map, right! Say "Map!"

Go over the Troll Bridge and across Sneezing Snake Lake to get to Rainy Mountain!

Here's the Troll Bridge. The Grumpy Old Troll
won't let us cross unless we solve his puzzle.
There are some pieces missing from the Bridge.
We need to put the right colour pieces back.
Some are green, verde, and some are blue, azul.
Let's say the colour of each piece in Spanish.
Verde, verde, azul, azul. They're in a pattern!

Now let's put the missing pieces back.
What colour is the first missing piece? Azul, right!
What about the second missing piece? ¡Verde!
Great – we solved the Grumpy Old Troll's puzzle
and now we can cross over the Troll Bridge.

Where do we go next? Sneezing Snake Lake! Do you see it anywhere? Yes, there it is. Do we need to follow the red path or the yellow path? The yellow path, right!

Here we are at Sneezing Snake Lake. How will we get across? We need to find a boat. Do you see a boat anywhere? Hey, there's one! But the boat is missing some of its colour.

What colour do we need to paint the boat? Red, right - rojo! Arco Iris can fill in the missing colour. Now let's paint the ends of the oars. What colour should we paint them? Yes, yellow. ¡Amarillo!

Do you see Swiper? Yes, there he is! He'll try and swipe the boat. Say "Swiper, no swiping" three times to stop him taking it. Well done, you stopped him!

Now let's row across the Lake. We need to row really fast to get past the snakes! Move your arms backwards and forwards like you're rowing. Keep going – that's it!

Count the number of snakes. Say "Achoo!" when you see each one.

Achoo!

Achoo!

We made it all the way across Sneezing Snake Lake! Do you remember where we go next? Rainy Mountain, that's right! We need to hurry – the sun needs a rainbow right away!

37

Answer on page 69.

We made it to Rainy Mountain! But Arco Iris is dirty from the journey. We need to get him clean before he can shine in the sky. Let's see if an Explorer Star can help. Say "¡Estrella!" Hey, it's Slipperoony! He will make Arco Iris clean again.

Thanks Slipperoony. Now Arco Iris is really shiny and sparkly. He is ready to shine in the sky for the very first time. ¡Buena suerte, Arco Iris!

SPANISH

good luck
buena suerte
say 'BWEH-nah
soo-ER-tay'

38

To shine in the sky, Arco Iris has to stretch out big and wide. We need to help. Put your arms out and stretch out like a rainbow. Keep stretching – stretch as wide as you can. Wow, look at Arco Iris! Everyone can see his beautiful colours. We did it! Thanks for all your help.

Fantastic Gymnastics!

Dora is a gymnast! Follow the instructions to do gymnastics with her!

1

Stand up please!

Reach up as high as you can – try to touch the sky!

2

Stretch out your arms and legs to make a star shape.

3

Try to stand on one leg without falling over!

4

You're great at gymnastics!

Now twirl around in a circle. Well done!

Draw lines to put each missing piece of the jigsaw in the right place.

Answer on page 69.

Now Dora is doing gymnastics with her friends. They've won rosettes!
Follow the lines to find out which colour rosette each friend has won.

Answer on page 69.

You can have a rosette of your own! Write your name on the dotted line, then decorate the rosette with lots of bright patterns and colours.

This rosette is for:

. . . .

I love doing gymnastics!

The Lost City

¡Hola! We're putting up a sign about my teddy bear. He's lost. I miss him so much.

Hey, Map says he knows where my teddy bear is - in the Lost City. The Lost City is a place filled with all the toys and treasures that everyone has ever lost! We need to go there and find my teddy bear. Map will tell us the way.

Map says we need to go through the Number Pyramid and the Mixed-Up Jungle to get to the Lost City. So first let's go to the Number Pyramid!

Look, it's Azul. He looks sad. He has lost his whistle! Don't worry Azul, we'll find your whistle. I bet it's in the Lost City, too. Azul says he will give us a ride to the Number Pyramid.

Here we are at the Number Pyramid! We need to swing over to the other side on one of these vines. But which vine should we take? Hey, let's see what that blue screen says!

To know which vine is right for you, First count five and then add two!

So first we have to count five vines. Count with me! 1, 2, 3, 4, 5. Now we need to add two more. 1, 2. Let's count to see what number vine we have to take. 1, 2, 3, 4, 5, 6, 7. Five plus two equals seven! So let's swing on vine number seven.

We made it all the way through the Number Pyramid! Now let's go to the Mixed-Up Jungle.

47

Here's the Mixed-Up Jungle.
Wow, it really is mixed up!
We need to fix it before
we can go through.

Look at the
clouds. Do they
belong on the
ground? No!
Where do clouds
belong? In the
sky, right!

48

What is wrong with these trees? They're in the sky - and they're upside down, too! Let's put them back on the ground.

Do you see a fish? Yes, in the nest! A fish doesn't belong in a nest - that's silly! Point to where the fish should be. Yes, in the water.

We fixed the Mixed-Up Jungle. ¡Muy bien! Now we can go through it and find the Lost City.

SPANISH

very good
muy bien
say 'mwee bee-EHN'

49

The Lost City is behind this curtain. We need to make the curtain go up to get to the Lost City. Say "Up!" Nothing happened! Perhaps the curtain speaks Spanish. Let's ask it in Spanish. Say "¡Arriba!"

SPANISH

up
arriba
say 'ah-REE-ba'

Yay, the curtain went up! Now we can get to the Lost City. ¡Vámonos!

No one has ever found the Lost City before! Look at all the lost toys. I bet all the things our friends have lost are here.

Tick ✓ each thing when you find it in the picture!

Azul's whistle

Benny's bat

Isa's wheels

Tico's keys

Swiper's glove

Great, we found all our friends' lost things. But we still need to find my teddy bear. Look all around – do you see him? Yes, there he is! I'm so glad we found him. We did it! Thanks for all your help.

WE DID IT! ¡LO HICIMOS!

Magical Puzzles

Dora and Boots are exploring in the Magic Garden! Look at the pictures and circle the eight differences in picture 1.

2

The Magic Garden is full of giant flowers, flores!

SPANISH

flowers
flores
say 'FLOR-ess'

Answers on page 69.

53

Look at the flower and find the shadow that matches exactly.

2

3

1

4

5

There are fairies in the Magic Garden, too! Draw lines to match them into pairs.

Answers on page 69.

SPANISH
fantastic
fantástico
say
'fahn-TAHS-tee-koh'

Flap your arms like a fairy's wings. ¡Fantástico!

Big Sister Dora

¡Hola! Today I have some really exciting news about my family. I can't wait to tell my friend Boots. Let's call him. Say "Boots!" Do you see Boots anywhere? Yes, there he is!

SPANISH

baby
bebé
say 'beh-BAY'

Do you want to hear my news? Somebody is going to join my family. They sleep in a cradle and wear a nappy. Can you guess who it is? A baby, right! My mami is going to have a baby – un bebé. And I'm going to be a big sister!

Hey, my phone is ringing. It might be Papi, with news about the baby! Will you find my phone in Backpack? Thanks!

"Beep beep!"

"Honk honk!"

"Tweet tweet!"

"Ring ring!"

Say each noise out loud. Which shape is the phone under? The triangle, right!

It's Papi. He says Mami is having the baby right now! We need to get home as quickly as we can. Let's find the fastest way to my house. Say "Map!"

Map says we go through the Spooky Forest and through the Nut Farm to get to my house. I wonder if the baby will be a boy or a girl? I can't wait to find out! Where do we go first? The Spooky Forest, right.

57

Now let's go to the Nut Farm! Do you see the Nut Farm? Yes, there it is – but it is very far away. Hey, there's Benny with his go-kart. He will give us a ride to the Nut Farm. But first he needs to put his go-kart together! Let's help.

We need to put the tyres, seat and steering wheel on Benny's go-kart. Let's put on the tyres. Twist your hands to put them on! Great.

Now let's push the seat on. Put your hands out in front of you and push down. That's it! Which part is left? The steering wheel! Let's twist it on. We did it, we fixed Benny's go-kart! Now he can give us a ride to the Nut Farm.

Here's the Nut Farm. It's really busy! The squirrels are collecting nuts. The traffic wardens have signs to show if the road is clear. Red means stop, and green means go!

Find your way through the Nut Farm by going down the roads with green signs!

Start

60

Finish

Great – we made it through the Nut Farm! We're almost at my house, mi casa!

SPANISH

my house
mi casa
say 'me KA-sa'

61

We made it to my house. I wonder if the baby has come. Papi says there is a really big surprise. Do you think the baby is a girl or a boy? Let's look and see ...

Wow, there are two babies. Twins! A baby girl AND a baby boy. I have a baby sister and a baby brother – una hermana y un hermano. They're so cute!

The babies are tired. We need to rock them to sleep. Will you help us rock them to sleep? Great! Make a cradle with your arms and rock them from side to side. Now sing your favourite lullaby! The babies are asleep – well done. We did it! Thanks for helping.

WE DID IT!
¡LO HICIMOS!

Bedtime Puzzles

It's time for Dora to go to bed. Read the rhyme, and when you see a picture, say the word out loud!

The has been shining in the sky,

But now he has to say goodbye.

The and are out instead,

It's time for me to go to  .

I'll brush my teeth and comb my hair,

And choose the I want to wear.

I'll climb into and hug my  ,

Then call to my to say I'm ready!

She'll read me a then turn off the ,

It's time to go to sleep - good night!

Help Dora get ready for bed. Tick ✓ the circle next to each thing she needs.

What's your favourite bedtime story?

Answers on page 69.

Boots is getting ready for bed, too! Join the dots to finish his pyjamas. Draw a pattern on them then colour in the picture.

Dora is fast asleep! Draw in what you think she is dreaming about. Say "Sweet dreams, Dora! ¡Dulces sueños!"

SPANISH

sweet dreams
dulces sueños
say 'DUL-sess
SWEN-yoss'

Dora did lots of things today! Write in the numbers from 1 to 3 to put the pictures in the right order.

Good night.
¡Buenos noches!

SPANISH
good night
buenos noches
say 'BWEH-nahs NOH-chays'

Answers on page 69.

Answers

Page 41

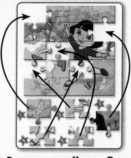

Page 16-17

Tico goes in his plane, Benny goes in his balloon and Isa goes on her scooter.

Page 18

Page 19 Pictures 1 and 4 are the same.

Page 21 The snowsuits and mittens will keep Dora and Boots warm.

Page 23

Page 28 Dora should take the apple, cupcake, sandwich and blanket.

Page 29 There are eight birds.

Page 30

Page 31 Path 2 leads to the nuts.

Page 37 There are five snakes.

Page 42 Dora - yellow, Boots - blue, Isa - pink, Tico - green.

Page 52-53

Page 54 Number 2 is the matching shadow.

Page 55

Page 58 There are five bats.

Page 60

Page 65 Dora needs her teddy, nightie, toothbrush and book.

Page 68

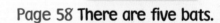

The blue bugs are on pages 9, 12, 18, 21, 30, 35, 44, 49, 55 and 67.

Have you seen the Dora Magazine?

ON SAL
every 3
weeks!

FREE Frog Game!

PLUS
Extra game
inside!

NICKELODEON
DORA
the
EXPLORER™

Issue
53

FRE
fabulou
gift ever
issue!

Exciting
puzzles

Pull-out
posters

Spot fairy differences

Sing rhymes with Dora

Follow Dora into a magical world!

Great
colouring

Join Dora in her exciting adventures with this fantastic magazine from Egmont

Available in all good retailers now!